This book belongs to:

Jennifer

Fieu

Berryland
Books

Edited by Claire Black
Illustrated by Eric Kincaid

Published by Berryland Books
www.berrylandbooks.com

First published in 2004

ISBN 1-84577-070-6
Printed in China

Jack
and the Beanstalk

Reading should always be FUN !

Reading is one of the most important skills your child will learn. It's an exciting challenge that you can enjoy together.

Treasured Tales is a collection of stories that has been carefully written for young readers.

Here are some useful points to help you teach your child to read.

Try to set aside a regular quiet time for reading at least three times a week.

Choose a time of the day when your child is not too tired.

Plan to spend approximately 15 minutes on each session.

Select the book together and spend the first few minutes talking about the title and cover picture.

Spend the next ten minutes listening and encouraging your child to read.

Always allow your child to look at and use the pictures to help them with the story.

Spend the last couple of minutes asking your child about what they have read. You will find a few examples of questions at the bottom of some pages.

Understanding what they have read is as important as the reading itself.

Once upon a time there was a young boy called Jack who lived with his mother.

They lived in a small house and were very poor.

One day Jack's mother asked Jack to take Daisy, their cow, to market and sell her for the highest price.

Jack really liked Daisy, but he did as his mother said.

Jack set off to market.

What is the cow called?

On his way, he met an old man who asked him where he was going.

"I'm off to the market to sell my cow, Daisy," Jack replied.

The old man asked Jack if he would exchange Daisy for some magic beans.

"No," replied Jack "my mother has asked me to take Daisy to the market to be sold."

"These magic beans will make you a rich man," claimed the old man.

Jack quickly changed his mind.

He exchanged Daisy for the beans and ran home to tell his mother.

Jack's mother was very angry.

She opened the window and threw the beans outside.

Jack was sent to bed without any supper.

Where did Jack's mother throw the beans?

That night, the magic beans began to grow and grow.

When Jack woke up the next morning, he opened the window and saw a tall beanstalk reaching up into the clouds.

He was so excited that he ran outside and began to climb up.

Jack climbed and climbed until he reached the top.

At the top there was a path leading to a giant castle.

When Jack reached the castle, he knocked on the huge front door.

A lady opened the door and then hurried Jack inside.

"Quickly, quickly, the giant is coming!" she said.

She then helped Jack to hide inside a cupboard.

The giant boomed,

"Fee-fi-fo-fum,
I smell the blood of an Englishman.

Be he alive, or be he dead,
I'll grind his bones to make my bread."

"Where is he, wife?" he shouted.

Who can the giant smell?

"There's no one here," she replied.

"Well then, fetch me my money bags!" he shouted.

The giant sat counting his golden coins and soon fell asleep.

Jack crept out from the cupboard, went over to the table and took some coins.

Then he ran out of the castle and down the beanstalk as quickly as he could.

When he arrived home his mother was so happy to see him and the golden coins.

They were no longer poor and had plenty to eat.

However, they soon ran out of money and were poor again.

Jack decided to climb the beanstalk once more.

Up he climbed into the clouds and followed the path to the castle.

The giant's wife was very frightened when she saw him.

"The giant was very angry last time you stole his gold coins," she said.

"I don't think I should let you come inside again."

Suddenly, the ground began to shake.

"You foolish boy, come inside and hide once more," she whispered.

Who is making the ground shake?

The giant roared,

"Fee-fi-fo-fum,

I smell the blood of an Englishman.

Be he alive, or be he dead,

I'll grind his bones to make my bread."

"Don't be so silly, come and enjoy your meal," said his wife.

After his meal he called for his golden hen.

"Lay, my special hen, lay," the giant said.

Each time he said 'Lay', the hen laid a beautiful golden egg.

Jack looked out from underneath the table, where he was hiding, to watch.

Once again the giant fell fast asleep at the table.

Jack crept up, stole the hen and climbed down the beanstalk as quickly as he could.

His mother couldn't believe it as each time Jack said 'Lay', the hen laid a golden egg.

Now they had all the gold they would ever need!

But Jack became greedy and he decided to climb the beanstalk again.

The giant's wife did not want to let him in.

The ground began to shake and Jack hid once more.

The giant asked for his golden harp and then he roared,

"Fee-fi-fo-fum,
I smell the blood of an Englishman.

Be he alive, or be he dead,
I'll grind his bones to make my bread."

His wife asked the harp to play a tune and soon the giant fell asleep.

Jack jumped up onto the table and grabbed the harp.

As he ran out of the castle the harp called out "Master! Master!"

The giant woke up and came thundering after Jack.

What did Jack steal this time?

Jack raced down the beanstalk as fast as he could.

He called out to his mother "Quick Mother, bring me an axe!

The giant is chasing after me!"

What did Jack ask his mother to bring?

Jack's mother rushed into the house and came out with an axe.

Jack grabbed the axe.

He swung the axe at the beanstalk and it came crashing down.

The giant also fell down to the ground and died at once.

Now Jack and his mother were safe and were never poor again.